UNSPOKEN

A STORY FROM THE

UNDERGROUND RAILROAD

Henry Cole

SCHOLASTIC PRESS — NEW YORK

TO A LIBRARIAN FRIEND,

WHO LONG AGO IGNITED THE SPARK

THAT LIT THE LANTERN

—*H.E.*

AUTHOR'S NOTE ⁓ When I was very little, I sat at the dining room table during Christmas and Thanksgiving dinners, and listened to elderly relatives tell Civil War stories—stories they had heard directly from people who had lived during the war! They told stories about hiding hams under the bedroom floorboards so marauding soldiers wouldn't find them—and how the greasy hams made the kitchen ceiling below impossible to paint for years and years. There were stories about great-aunts who were forced to bake bread for enemy troops, and who would spit into the bread dough as a way of retaliating. There was even a great-grandfather who took a minié ball in his leg at the Battle of Seven Pines.

WE LIVED ON a dairy farm in Loudoun County, Virginia. The soil of that particular part of Virginia is especially good for agriculture, with its deep, rich band of loam beneath gently rolling hills and Goose Creek meandering through—perfect for raising crops and grazing cattle. But from 1861 to 1865 those same hills were continually trampled and scarred as the American Civil War left its impact on the countryside.

Our farm was about equidistant between Manassas, Virginia—where the battles of Bull Run took place— about thirty miles to the southeast, and Sharpsburg, Maryland—where the Battle of Antietam was fought— about thirty miles to the northwest. Bull Run was where one of the most decisive battles of the Civil War was fought. And Antietam was the bloodiest one-day battle in American history, with roughly 23,000 casualties.

Loudoun County, bordered on the north by the Potomac River, was at the edge of the Confederacy. Because of its proximity to the North, the people of this county were divided in their allegiances. Sometimes friends fought against friends, brothers against brothers.

IF YOU WERE an escaped slave in this area, your chances of making it north of Virginia were greatly increased if you knew of "safe houses," houses of sympathetic Southerners who hid and fed escapees and helped them find safe travel northward.

Also, runaways who could locate and identify Polaris, the North Star, were able to continue their journey in a safe direction. Polaris is a fixed point in the northern sky, while other stars seem to revolve around it. Because of its position near the Big Dipper (which is easy to spot) it has been used for centuries as a guide, pointing the way for nighttime travelers. If, on a clear night, a runaway slave could find Polaris, he or she knew the direction north—toward freedom.

MY HOME NOW, in Virginia, has the tumbled remains of an old stone wall running through the woods where, I have heard, a small Civil War skirmish occurred. Almost every day, I am reminded of the events that have happened around me during that war. It's not so surprising that I wanted to create a picture book that was evocative of that era.

But I didn't want this story to tell about bloody battles or spitting into bread dough. I wanted to tell—or show—the courage of everyday people who were brave in quiet ways.

I wanted to make this a wordless book. The two main characters in the story are both brave, have a strong bond, and communicate with great depth. Yet, both are silent. They speak without words.

Because I made only the pictures, I'm hoping you will write the words and make this story your own—filling in all that has been *unspoken*.

LIBRARY OF CONGRESS CATALOGING-IN-PUBLICATION DATA Cole, Henry, 1955– Unspoken : a story from the Underground Railroad / by Henry Cole. — 1st ed. p. cm. Summary: In this wordless picture book, a young Southern farm girl discovers a runaway slave hiding behind the corn crib in the barn and decides to help him. ISBN 978-0-545-39997-5 (hardcover : alk. paper) 1. Underground Railroad—Fiction. [1. Underground Railroad—Fiction. 2. Fugitive slaves—Fiction. 3. African Americans— Fiction.] I. Title PZ7.C67345Un 2012 [E]—dc23 2011043583 • 10 9 8 7 6 5 4 3 2 1 12 13 14 15 16 • Printed in Singapore 46 • First edition, November 2012 • The display type was set in ITC Esprit Bold and P22 Cezanne Regular. • The text was set in Adobe Garamond Pro Regular. • The artwork was done on Canson charcoal paper with Staedtler Mars 4B pencils. • Art direction and book design by Marijka Kostiw